COMPLICATED

ASHLYN MATHEWS

Copyright © 2019 by Ashlyn Mathews

Previously published title: Secrets and Lies

All rights reserved. No part of this publication may be reproduced, distributed or transmitted in any form or by any means without the prior written permission of the publisher.

Publisher's Note: This is a work of fiction. Names, characters, places, and incidents are a product of the author's imagination. Locales and public names are sometimes used for atmospheric purposes. Any resemblance to actual people, living or dead, or to businesses, companies, events, institutions, or locales is completely coincidental.

Complicated/Ashlyn Mathews -- 1st ed.

❧ Created with Vellum

"This above all: to thine own self be true. And it must follow, as the night the day, thou canst not then be false to any man."

~ William Shakespeare, Hamlet

1

EMERSYN

"Emmie, are you sure you'll be all right?"

My best friend, Andy, shoots me furtive, worried glances. She's helping load my luggage in my car.

"Why wouldn't I be? I'm going home." I load the last of my luggage in the trunk before I hoist Charlie, my more-pudge-than-stocky English bulldog, onto the front passenger seat.

I close the door, and he does something I find utterly adorable. Charlie grabs hold of the open window and runs his big paws along the edge, like he's playing the piano. I laugh, and he gives me a toothy, slobbery grin. This dog… I scratch behind his ear.

"You haven't been back since you left for college, Em."

Andy and I met our freshman year and hit it off right away.

I give Charlie another good scratch behind his ear. "The wonders of technology, right?" Grandpa and I FaceTime. "My grandfather said Pandora hasn't changed since I left."

"And that's what worries me." The lines on Andy's forehead deepen. "Move your grandpa here until he recovers. There's more than enough room."

Andy inherited money when her parents died in a car accident last year. She used the money to buy a huge home with a mother-in-law apartment on the lower level that I rent.

"I don't want to impose."

"We're *best friends*," she says with finality in her tone, as though friendship is the answer for all my problems.

Returning home is about more than helping my grandfather with life after hip replacement surgery. I hope time in Pandora will force me to shut the door on my past.

"What if *he's* there?"

He is Six. Reed "Six" Haider. Six-foot-one. Lean.

Jet-ink hair. Royal blue eyes. The bane of my existence. The star of my sexual fantasies. Out of my league.

I lift my hair off my neck and swipe at the beads of sweat on my forehead. It's another hot August day.

"I doubt it. The last I heard, he's on the road for an away game." My grandfather brings up Reed a lot.

"Last *I* heard, he's on a five-game suspension for getting into a fight with the umpire over a bad call. That's not like him. Nothing fazes Reed on the field."

Andy would know. She's a huge baseball fan.

"Maybe he'll use the time for some R&R, spending it poolside at his *sprawling* house in Cali, surrounded by silicone," I volunteer.

The thought of him with other women rankles me, a reaction that hasn't diminished over the years.

"Is that something the guy you hooked-up with would do? From what little you told me, Reed is a good guy with substance and old-fashioned values."

Reed was more than a hook-up. He was my first crush and my first love. He took a chance on me. Made me happy.

Things were fine until I told lies and kept secrets from him. We broke up, and a week later, Reed left town to attend an out-of-state college on a full-ride scholarship. I haven't seen him since.

I lean against the car door and sigh.

"I have no clue. I was just putting the thought out there. How he lives his life is none of my business. I listen to my grandfather brag, but I don't go looking."

Andy's eyes widen. "You *haven't* searched him online since he left Pandora to play at UCLA?"

"He moved on. I did, too."

"You haven't. I can tell."

"How?" I challenge, raising my brow.

Andy is a keen observer of human behavior. I think her perceptiveness is from growing up under the suspicion she had something to do with her sister's disappearance.

"There's the faraway look in your eyes when you FaceTime your grandfather, and he goes on and on about the homegrown star. There's the fire in your eyes just now at the thought of Reed *commiserating* with half-naked women with fake boobs."

Darn it, she's onto me.

"Em, what will you do if he's in Pandora?"

This girl is *persistent*.

Charlie paws my back, pestering for me to haul butt. He's impatient and excited. He's looking forward to the a/c blowing in his face. He also wants to stick his broad head out the window. There's so much to see and smell on the drive out of town. To be a dog. What a life.

"I'll deal with it if it happens."

"Living on the fly." Andy flips her long, chestnut-brown hair over her shoulder. "I'm surprise you saved enough money to rent a place for a month. That takes planning."

"It had less to do with planning and more to surprise you with," I tease, tossing her words at her. "Shows you I'm capable of change with the right prodding." Friendship, laughter, understanding, to name a few, and Andy just being there for me.

"The more things change, the more they stay the same." My grandfather's favorite saying rings true for me.

I'm not the same person I was when I left home. I have friends, including a BFF that's a girl. Growing up, girls my age avoided me.

I also have someone other than my grandfather that loves me unconditionally. I glance over my shoulder. Charlie tips his face up and gives me another toothy, slobbery grin. He's a good dog, and a great friend.

Yet the more I changed, the more I stayed the

same. Beneath the surface of my change, I'm the insecure teenage girl looking for approval and acceptance after growing up with the invisible stamp of "dirty" on my forehead for my father's unthinkable sin.

No wonder my last relationship didn't work.

I shove thoughts of my ex into the corner of my mind, alongside thoughts of my parents. I have no clue where they are, and my grandfather had long ago cut ties with his ex-wife and their daughter after Grandfather found out my grandmother cheated on him and had a child with another man. My mother's half-brother is two years older than her.

Imagine my grandfather's surprise when my mom dropped me off at his doorstep and ran off with her latest boyfriend. I was twelve.

Charlie head-butts me, reminding me I don't need my parents' love. I have Charlie and Andy. They love and accept me for who I am. I straighten my shoulders, refusing to let the circumstance of my birth define who I am as a person. My father's sin is not *my* sin.

"I should get going." I have a seven-hour drive ahead of me. "I'll text when I get there."

I'll be in Pandora around dinner time. Perfect.

Grandpa texted asking me to pick up fried chicken, coleslaw, and mashed potatoes before he starts his culinary theme for the month. Yum.

"Promise you won't let their actions hurt you?"

I confessed to Andy how the kids bullied me while their parents looked down their noses at me. Except for Reed's family.

They were nothing but kind to my grandfather and me. Until one night of lies and secrets destroyed how I saw Reed's perfect family. They weren't. They had dark and sinful secrets, too, except my family's secret was in the open for people to ridicule and whisper over.

"Promise you'll come back the same Emersyn Collins that had me laughing so hard I peed my pants?"

Andy is such a good friend. Kind-hearted. Fiercely protective. Another reason our friendship works. After the shit I went through as a kid, kind-hearted and fiercely protective was what I needed most to believe in the power of friendship again.

I pull her in for a hug, missing her already. "I promise. Thank you for always being there for me."

Andy was there when I ended things with my boyfriend after he cheated on me with his secretary.

(How cliché.) Andy was with me when I got a dog. Anything to take away the crushing weight of Scott's betrayal. Andy was also around when Charlie cried in the middle of the night or early morning to be let out to do his duty.

Taking care of a puppy was more difficult than starting a business, but Charlie is worth it. As though he knows he's on my mind, Charlie runs a trail of slobber up and down my bare arm. Wet kisses from my one-year-old cutie pie. I smile and let go of Andy before she gets a tongue bath, too.

"Will *you* be okay?" I ask.

Her brows tug low. "A month without you will be weird. Who will I binge-watch Netflix shows with? Who will go with me to hot yoga? Or help me pick deadheads off the flowers?" The flower garden in the back of the house.

After graduating from Pendleton University in southwestern Washington state, Andy and I stayed put and opened a catering business.

"A month will fly by. Anyway, you're not getting rid of me so easily. We'll FaceTime. And I plan on being online every chance I get. Where I go, so does my dandy phone and laptop." My cell in my hand, I wave and climb inside my car.

Andy disappears in my rearview mirror. I smile and turn on the music.

Owning a business with my best friend is a dream I never thought possible. Not after the life I lived back in Pandora.

2

EMERSYN

To get to Pandora, there's a bridge to cross. Below me is the Raging River.

I drive on the bridge and over the dried-up river, recalling my car ride here. It would be the final time my mother pawned me off to family. When she told me where we were going, I right away searched up Greek mythology on Pandora's box.

According to mythology, curiosity got the better of Pandora, and she opened the box, releasing the bad into the world but locking hope inside when she realized her mistake and closed the box.

Pandora is where I suffered. Pandora is also where I learned to hope for something better. I tied my hope to one man—Reed Haider.

Twenty-minutes from my grandfather's property,

Charlie whines. He only whines on car rides when he needs to do his duty.

"I know just the place. Hang tight, Charlie Brown." I pull into the back lot of Raging River Bar, park, and run around to the passenger-side door.

Charlie bolts out before I can put a collar and leash on him. Weaving my fingers through my hair, I blow out a breath and follow Charlie to the open field behind the bar.

I don't like when he runs off, but when he has to go, Charlie *has* to go. I glance around. It's five o'clock on a Wednesday, and from the looks of the near-empty parking lot, people aren't ready to hit up the bar until way later, if at all.

There shouldn't be any harm in letting him free-roam.

While Charlie does his thing, I text Andy I'm in Pandora. Then I let my grandfather know I'll be at his place soon with food. He sends back the thumbs-up emoji. I set my cell in the cupholder and rummage in my glove compartment for a poop bag.

I find one and pick up Charlie's pile. Just my luck a squirrel chooses that moment to skitter down the tree next to us and scurries across the parking lot. Charlie takes off running on his short legs.

I run after him, holding the bag of poop.

"Charlie Brown, you get back here right now!" He's not listening. "Charlie Brown!"

Two things happen simultaneously. The squirrel beats feet up a light pole. Charlie comes to a dead stop and barks. The door of the bar swings open. Masculine laughter. I pivot my attention to the familiar sound.

Reed. Six. Reed Haider is walking out of the bar, his arms slung across the shoulders of two beautiful women in tight mini-dresses and sky-high heels. I can't stop staring. He is as hot at twenty-five as he was when he was eighteen. When he was mine.

We met in secret and talked. Made love, too. We were like Romeo and Juliet, and just like their story, ours took a tragic turn.

His laughter fades, and he stares back at me. His arms fall from the women's shoulders, and he glowers. Reed is still angry with me. He hasn't forgiven me for what I professed to have done that night, the night that shattered us and our plans to be together. The night his mom lost her life.

The force of his anger slams into me, and my body stills. I can't draw enough air into my lungs. My head spins. I can't move or speak. At my side, Charlie senses something is off. He snarls and bares his teeth.

And I... I relive the night that changed *everything*.

Rain pounding on my face.

Loud voices from the cliffside.

Oh, God, he's hurting her.

I raise my voice above the relentless rain. "Stop, please. She's too close to the edge."

Rough hands on my arms shoving me away.

Small, slender fingers grasping for mine.

The look of horror on his face.

The expression of fear on hers.

I reach for her. *We* reach for her. But it's too late. She's fallen over the edge and into the darkness.

A string of curses followed by a man yelling my name rips me out of my nightmare. I blink. Charlie has a firm hold on Reed's ankle. The women have taken refuge in Reed's pickup truck.

I rush over and tap Charlie on the top of his head. "Let go, buddy. It's time to just. Let. Go."

Charlie listens, and with a backwards glance my way, he trots to the car and plops his butt in front of the door. He's ready to go.

Too bad, so sad. There's damage control to take care of. I get on my haunches and raise my gaze to Reed.

"Do you mind?" I grab the hem of his jeans.

Brows angled low, Reed shakes his head. I lift his

pants leg and pull down his sock, avoiding touching him.

"He didn't break skin." I thought so. I pull up Reed's sock and lower his pants leg. "Charlie is more of a lover than a fighter. His bites are love bites." I stand. "He's harmless."

"He might be, but you're not. Stay the hell away from me, Emersyn." He glares and backs up toward his truck.

I straighten my shoulders and tip my chin at him. No matter how much his words hurt, I'll keep my promise to Andy. I won't let Reed distancing himself from me shred my insides to pieces.

"I'll do my best. Goodbye, Reed." I'm relieved my voice is steady, but I couldn't conceal the pleading in my tone, the memories from that night fresh on my mind.

Forgive me.

I'm sorry.

Sorry she died.

Sorry I couldn't save her.

If I could, I would take your mother's place in a heartbeat.

But the past is the past, and I can't change it no matter how many times I relive that moment in my mind and in my nightmares.

His steps falter, and for a moment, the anger fades from his face before he blinks, and the emotion reappears full force.

"Come on, Six. You promised us a good time back at your place," one of the women says out the window.

"Yeah, sure sweet thing. Six is all yours for the rest of the night."

I turn my back to him before he could see the tears in my eyes. Substance and old-fashioned values my ass. Money and fame changes people, Reed included. My throat constricts, and I hurry to my car. I couldn't care less if he's moved on with other women. Moving on is a part of life, right?

I blink at the tears and help Charlie into the car. He licks my face. I wrap my arms around him and hold him tight. Who could refuse unconditional love? Not this girl.

I let the tears fall and don't glance up until Reed drives out of the parking lot. It's been seven years since I've seen Reed, and seeing him again brings to the surface memories I've kept hidden in my mind, my own Pandora's box of destruction and…hope.

3
EMERSYN

After Grandpa and I catch up over dinner and watch a few episodes of "Stranger Things," I go over with him the do's and don'ts after hip replacement surgery. Grandpa can be stubborn, and one wrong move to prove he can dance the funky chicken could pop out his new hip.

"Are you sure you don't want to stay with your granddad? I still have my shotgun." He waggles his eyebrows.

I give his hand a gentle pat. "Thank you for being the overprotective grandpa, but I'm grown now and so are the kids that bullied me."

He scowls. "You might run into those grown bullies."

"Grandpa, I don't mind gettting your groceries and picking up your mail. Truly."

He's obsessed with cooking, online shopping, and my welfare.

"What's that second favorite line of yours?"

"Sticks and stones may break my bones, but words can never hurt me."

"Exactly."

He squeezes my hand. The love in his eyes… What would I have done and what kind of woman would I have become without my grandfather's unfaltering love and support growing up?

"What's your interest this month?"

Grandpa's culinary theme.

He eyes the leftover food I picked up from Roxy's Fried Chicken. "Clean ingredients. Back to basics."

"I like it." I stick up my hand, and we high-five.

I look past his shoulder. Charlie is snoozing by the television.

"Charlie won't give you any troubles." I sip my white wine.

Grandpa insisted Charlie stay the night. His golden retriever, Red, died two years ago.

"It'll be nice to have a dog around."

Before he decides whether to get one.

That's what I hear beneath the sadness and weariness in his voice.

"I should let you rest." I push back my chair. "I'll take Charlie out before I go."

I tuck his grocery list inside my bag.

"Grandpa, why do I need to get your mail and packages at the post office? Don't they deliver to your gate?"

"Not after I had a row with Eileen two months ago in the frozen food aisle."

Eileen Holton is the owner of the local post office.

"The mean things she said about your mother and uncle. I won't tolerate her judgment over something I had no control of. Kids these days are prone to being delinquent at an early age with as much crap as there is on the Internet."

He balls his hand.

"And she's still holding that damn grudge against me for taking a shot at her grandson."

I reach over and unfurl his fist. Everyone involved should take a deep breath and let go of the past. I plan on it before my month in Pandora is up.

"Would you mind if I ask Eileen to reconsider having the mail delivered to your gate, again? And she must realize you shooting at her grandson was a case of mistaken identity."

He huffs and puffs. "Missy, I can tell the difference between a mean-ass boy and a bear. That boy gave you the biggest grief."

"For crashing his dirt bike," when I was fifteen. "Granger got over it and treated me right when I told him I stole it back from the kid that stole it first."

"One exception does not make everything else right. I refuse to forgive the kids and their parents for doing wrong by you. You deserved none of their hate and scorn just because you were conceived from rape."

There's more to my conception than rape.

The past is the past, and I can't change it. But I can change my grandfather's way of thinking.

THE DRIVE from my grandfather's place to the small house I'm renting gives me the chance to think over his words before he headed for bed.

"Give the bullies an inch and they'll take a mile. Don't budge, Emersyn."

I don't plan on getting taken advantage of while

I'm here, but I would like to forgive and move on with my life. Except my life is tied to my grandfather's, and he isn't ready to let go. Unless he drinks the Kool-Aid I'm drinking.

I park in front of the rental and grab the keys from the lockbox.

I'll do more than help tend to my grandfather's property and run his errands. I'll show him forgiveness has the power to give him a fresh start with the people that had hurt me with their crude words and mean actions. My fresh start was refreshing, and what I needed most when I left Pandora for college.

Excited with my plan, I haul the last luggage inside the house. My neighbor's door opens. Loud music spills out. High-pitched giggling. Deep, masculine laughter. I groan in my mouth.

No wonder the pickup truck in the driveway next to my rental looked familiar.

Reed walks out of the house with a dark-haired beauty clinging to his throwing arm. I must have made a noise. He glances my way. The woman's giggles fade when she sees me, and her attention swivels to my car, no doubt wondering where my mean AF lovebug, Charlie Brown, is hiding.

I tip my chin, walk inside, and close the door.

There's no sense making another scene, but yeah, I wanted to rush over and rip the sexy brunette's arm from around Reed's.

I lean against the door, my heart beating out of control. Good God, what is wrong with me? Reed is not *my* guy. I roll my luggage into the bedroom. Unbecoming panic settles on my chest. This can't be happening.

Reed is my neighbor?

Two thoughts cross my mind.

One, Andy must never find out. I'll never hear the last of it. Two, I hope Reed keeps his stay short. I don't think I can handle seeing him go in and out of the house with a different woman hanging on his arm without wishing I had the superpower to hurl the house and its occupants elsewhere.

Sighing at my crummy luck, I unpack my laptop on the kitchen table and start working on the project I'm in charge of—a fancy dinner for Pendleton University's staff and their families, a-welcome-back, we-appreciate-you type of affair.

I bring up the dean's request on my laptop and lay out paper menus on the table. The music and laughter drifting from next door is loud, the single pane windows of the rental poor barriers of outside noise.

A headache starts at the back of my head and moves to my temples and my forehead, creating a tight band. I rub at my temples. I can't think and it's sweltering hot.

I stand and pace, hoping to get air moving beneath my clothes without resorting to getting bare-ass naked. Tomorrow, I'll pick up a floor fan at the hardware store. I won't let Andy down by letting my headaches, nightmares, and Reed's anger stop me from doing my best work.

Starting a catering business and naming it in her sister's memory was Andy's idea. I went along for the ride because she's my BFF, and I know how much she loved and misses her sister.

The headache doesn't go away. I'm sweating. I need fresh air. Shoving my cell in the back pocket of my shorts and the house keys in the front pocket, I decide a walk to one of my favorite spots will do me good. It's dark, but I'm not afraid.

There aren't wild animals like bears and cougars in Pandora. And I've taken self-defense classes and kick-boxing classes since my freshman year of college. Andy's idea.

I head out and lock the door behind me.

Being near my favorite spots and my grandfather's

property was the reason I settled on this rental. But I wouldn't have signed the agreement had I known Reed would be next door. It's too late to change that now.

The trail I used to get to the spot by the creek runs along the back of the only two houses on this street. The easiest and quickest way to get there without getting attacked by blackberry bushes is to walk between the houses and behind the house Reed is staying in.

I pace in the driveway with my arms crossed.

When I contacted the rental management company, they assured me the home next door was empty, though it took the woman a few days to get back to me after I gave her my name. I didn't want to traipse through the yard if someone was staying in the house. I would take the long way around, bypassing the blackberries.

Perturbed with my surprise neighbor, I make up my mind and traipse through the yard. Walking between the houses, I keep my gaze front and center. Nothing but silence. What happened with the music? Curious, I turn my head.

Bad idea.

Reed is in the kitchen washing his hands. Slender arms circle his broad shoulders from behind. Fiery red manicured nails. He raises his eyes and meets mine.

Time stops.

I stop.

My heart beats out of control.

I stare.

I don't blink.

I remember how he used to look at me.

Tenderness in his eyes when he told me how special I am to him. His royal blue eyes darkening with desire when we made love for the first time. Excitement in them when he told me UCLA offered him a full-ride scholarship to play ball.

Then that night happened and all I see is anger in his eyes. And the god-awful words he said to me at his mother's funeral…

"Why'd you come here, Emersyn? You disrespect my memories of my mother with your presence. Get the fuck out of here. You don't belong."

I blink, and time returns to normal.

Tears blur my vision, and I tear my gaze from his, hurrying away from the satisfaction on his face at seeing the remorse on mine.

Forgive me.

I'm sorry.

Sorry she died.

Sorry I couldn't save her.

If I could, I would take your mother's place in a heartbeat.

I repeat the words etched on my heart and in my mind.

Why did I believe returning home would be easy? I hug myself. It's because I hadn't expected Reed to be in town.

4
REED

The hurt in Emersyn's eyes and the remorse on her face gnaw at me, and I can't do it. I can't make these women's dream come true.

"Sorry, ladies, but baking pecan pies will have to wait another day."

"But we heard your pies are to die for. Something to do with the nuts you use."

I clear my throat. This conversation is taking a turn for the worse. Down the front of my pants worse. I see the way the women look at me with hunger in their eyes. I notice them checking out my crotch.

"That's 'nut.' Singular. One kind of nut. Pecan. Sorry to cut the fun short. My friend, Granger, will drive you two back to your hotel."

I text Granger. I hate to impose on him; it's his day off. But after what he *withheld* from me, I'm entitled to imposing on his time. He rolls up in his big-ass truck ten minutes later.

I open the door. "Good night, ladies."

"Will we see you again?"

Hope flares in their eyes only to die when I tell them, "No." I shouldn't start anything with my fans.

They climb inside Granger's truck.

My cell belts out Garth Brooks' "Friends in Low Places." I answer. "Yeah, man?"

"Reason better be good for calling in a favor."

The line goes dead. Granger sticks his arm out the driver-side window and waves.

I close the door and pace.

What was Granger thinking renting the house his mother willed to him to Emersyn? Why didn't he tell me she'd be in Pandora the same time as me? He knew I would be staying next door. He owns this house, too. Bought it outright with the money he inherited from his mom.

I shove my fingers in my hair and yank at the strands. Why am I pissed? Granger doesn't have to tell me jack shit. His property. His business.

Still… Seeing Emersyn again dredges up long-buried emotions. Regret. Hurt. Disbelief. Deep. Seated. Anger.

I've carried my anger for her below the surface for so long, I'm ready to let it go. Letting go in the form of popping off at the umpire and taking a shot at him with my fist wasn't the wisest move. Something's got to give, and I won't let it be my career.

I have to let go of my anger for Emersyn. I have to stop worrying I'll spout mean and hateful words to her. I'll treat her decent, but it doesn't mean I forgive her for her part in my mother's death.

My mind made up, I follow my gut-instinct. My gut-instinct pans out when I catch sight of her at our secret spot. The big trees at our back that line the dirt path conceal us.

She's sitting on a log set back from the creek. Her butt is half-on, half-off the log, and she has her arms outstretched behind her. She tips her face to the moon and her profile is as graceful as the first time I spotted her here, when something sparked and started between us.

Emersyn's dark hair isn't cropped to her chin, but falls past her shoulders. Her breasts are fuller than when she was fifteen. Slim waist. Slender legs. Thin and small as before to my six-foot-one build.

Her shoulders shake. Her sobs hit me deep in my core. I take a step and another.

"Red light. Don't you come any closer, Reed Gareth Haider."

Red light, green light—one game we played when we met in secret. She faces me. Creamy, smooth skin. Pert nose. Full, red lips. I can't stop staring. She's beautiful. Have grown more beautiful with the passing of time.

She raises her chin. "Yeah, I'm an ugly crier. Don't rub it in, okay?"

"Emers." I take another step.

"I said red light, Reed." She stands and balls her fists against her sides. "Or is it Six? How could you? That was between us. What…" Her chin tips higher. "What you are to me."

What I am to her.

What she is to me.

What we had—happiness and hope.

Until Emersyn destroyed me with what she did to my mom.

Her tears fall, and I shield my heart from her hurt. She has no right to shed tears for us.

"I believed in you. Believed your lucky number would take you far."

Six. My jersey's number through high school.

"And it did, all the way to the top. You're playing in the Majors, Reed. Your dream came true."

"And yours didn't…One?"

She was my number one girl. The only one for me. So much so I was willing to take her wherever I went. That was our dream. Her dream. To not be stuck in Pandora.

She smiles through her tears, and my breath catches in my throat with how beautiful she is with the moon high in the sky.

"They did. I left Pandora in one piece."

"Not so." I swallow past the rock-size lump in my throat. "You left a piece of yourself behind, right here."

I set my palm over my heart and reinforce the shield I placed over it, knowing what my next words will be.

"I want to return it to you."

Her sobs pierce the air, and my gut clenches.

"Ending things between us is the right thing to do, Emers. Telling you it's over will give me closure and help me move on."

"What you said is seven years too late, you had no troubles moving on without me, and fine, so we're done. Anything else?" she ticks off on her fingers.

"I want us to talk."

"Here?" Her shoulders slump. Crestfallen expression.

"Why not here?" I will myself to stay put. To not yank her into my arms and apologize over and over for being responsible for the hurt on her face.

"This was the spot you proposed, Reed. Or did you forget?"

"I didn't." I shove my hands in my pockets and pull my shoulders to my core. "I figured you would want a place to rest with the crying you've been doing. Crying is draining."

I did a lot of crying after my mom's death.

"Okay."

She sits.

"Green light."

I walk over and mimic her earlier pose.

"How's life? What have you been up to?" I go for casual and general.

"Life is good. Great."

She tips forward with her arms crossed. Long hair falls around her face, and she tucks the strands behind her ears.

"My friend and I graduated from Pendleton last year. We opened a catering business together. We live together, too. Andy is great. You?" She stares forward, not sparing me a glance.

"Same, except I graduated from UCLA. Play ball in the Majors. And... I live alone." I raise my hand, not sure why other than our talk reminds me of the first day of class, everyone having a turn telling something small but impersonal.

Except what Emersyn said isn't small or impersonal.

"So you're happy?" Happy with this Andy dude.

A "duh" question. Of course she's happy. According to Emersyn, life is great.

"I am. Thank you for asking."

She stands.

"I should go. I have an early morning and unfinished work waiting on my laptop and kitchen table."

She kicks at the grass.

"I'll try my best to stay far away from you. But if we run into one another again, I hope we can be civil, Reed. I'm not here to stir shit up. I'm here to help my grandfather. Will you do that, be civil?"

"I can. Should we shake on it?" I rise, taking up space in her personal space.

She steps back.

"Touching you isn't a good idea."

She bites down on her lower lip, drawing my

attention to her mouth. I gave Emersyn her first kiss. Was her first, too.

"I'm *happy*, Reed. Please understand."

Yeah, I get it. She's happy with this guy of hers. Jealousy I haven't felt in a long time claws at my heart.

"It's an innocent handshake, Emers." I extend my hand.

I'm a persistent son of a bitch, but persistence got me where I'm at, playing ball at the highest level. Will her hand in mine feel just as small, warm, and fragile as the first time we shook on agreeing to meeting again in secret?

She stares at my hand and glares.

"What part of 'I'm happy' don't you understand?" She barges past me. "It took me a long time to get over you. Don't ruin my happiness, Reed. Please, don't."

She runs off. The agony in her voice… I go after her. But her plead to not cause a ripple through her happiness… Blowing out a frustrated breath, I grab the nearest rock and chuck it at the creek.

I should forget Emersyn. I've said my piece. Have officially called off our engagement seven fucking years later. There's nothing more to say to her.

My anger and hurt should subside, but it doesn't. My emotions burn hotter than ever.

To get my closure and return to who I was before Emersyn's confession crushed me, I have to forgive her for what she did the night my mother lost her life.

Easier said than done.

5
EMERSYN

"Seriously, Andy, I can't believe you're calling me already. It hasn't even been twenty-four hours since we last saw one another."

Smiling, I grab the bag of chocolate chips off the counter and set it inside the wired shopping basket. Clean and back to basics is awesome. I like Grandpa's theme for this month, but what's missing from his list is dessert.

"Catch me up then. What have you done today?" Her voice comes in through my earbuds.

"First off, I can't believe I'm walking around the grocery store looking like I'm talking to myself. I swore I would never be one of those people going from aisle to aisle looking crazy as shit. What you have me doing."

She laughs. "I bet you look *ape-shit* crazy."

I narrow my eyes. "You called on purpose. You knew I would be running errands. No way will I wear a gorilla suit to Chloe's get-together."

"You made the bet, and you lost, Em."

"You have no proof."

"*Em.*"

She's trying not to laugh. I can hear her smile.

"Fine."

"What else will you be doing?" Her voice goes up a notch on "else."

Persistent to her core.

"I will take back *everything* I said about you and them," our friends, "being *obsessed* with AirPods."

Her laughter lightens my mood more.

"I'm so glad you called."

Our conversation is a great detractor, taking my mind off my short, but intense, interaction with Reed last night. God, I dislike that word. Makes what happened impersonal when it wasn't. But what happened wasn't a run-in or an agreed-upon meet-up, either. Reed at one of our secret spots was intentional.

He intended on ending "us."

"Okay, what have you done so far? Tell, tell, tell," Andy says in a sing-song voice.

I smile past the ache in my chest. "Are you sure? I'll bore you."

"The details will help me work better."

"Because you're multi-tasking and need to add my uneventful day to your pile?"

"Ugh, 'pile' sounds downright gross. But yes, add, add, add," she says in the same sing-song voice.

I laugh. This girl and her optimism.

"I love you, you know that?"

"I love you, too. Details, please."

I can hear her typing away at her computer.

"Well, I woke up at the butt crack of dawn and ran over to my grandfather's to take Charlie out. You know how he gets."

"Sure. When he has to go, he *has* to go."

I laugh. "I meant my grandfather. He's stubborn, and I was afraid he would take Charlie out and forget he's not supposed to bend at the waist to pick up Charlie's poo."

I grab a package of pasta off the shelf and read the list of ingredients on the back. Two items listed. Awesome. I set the box in my basket.

"Hey, when will I get to meet your grandfather in real life? And did you really *run* over?"

"FaceTime isn't enough? Yes, I did. I have to look

good for the wedding." Chloe's wedding. I'm a bridesmaid.

Lucky me, my cheating, lying ex is a groomsman.

"Technology isn't a substitute for a real connection, Emmie."

Don't I know it. The DMs on the dating apps I'm on are downright impersonal.

"Can I get back to you? Let me see how it goes while I'm here. If all's well, we can visit after the wedding."

Scott will be in Pendleton catching up with his college buddies. No way will I stick around town and watch him preen with his drop-dead gorgeous girlfriend—the secretary he cheated on me with—on his arm. We stayed friends with the same group of people after our breakup.

"That'll be great, Em."

"Awesome. We'll plan for it." I groan the second the words left my mouth.

"Emersyn Collins, first the running, then saving up money, and now you're making more plans?"

"Don't get used to it." I cruise over to the feminine products aisle and reach for a box of tampons. I glance at my grandfather's list to make sure I didn't miss something before I pay. I have what's on the list *and* extra.

"I should go, Andy. I love you. Miss you. Say 'hi' to the gang." I have great friends. Smiling, I swipe the box of tampons off the shelf and catch it with my basket.

Large boots stop in front of me. I raise my gaze. Dark denim. Higher. Navy blue T-shirt. Muscular, tan arms. Broad chest. Even higher. Reed stares back at me. Glances at what's in my basket. Cocks a brow.

Huh?

I look. A box of condoms sits atop the bag of chocolate chips. XXL, ribbed. My cheeks heat.

"Um, Andy I have to go." I cut her short, not realizing she's been talking to me. God, I'm a crappy friend.

"Is something wrong? You sound out of breath."

"Hey, Emersyn."

"Good god, that voice… Who is the sex-on-a-stick speaking to you? I swear my panties are wet."

I groan. "Reed."

"Holy shit, he's there? I told you so."

"Now is not the time to get sassy," I growl.

"Em—"

"Gotta go, Andy." I end our call, yank the Airpods from my ears, and drop them in my bag.

Hot from my hairline to my toes, I replace the

condoms I mistakenly grabbed with a box of mini-tampons.

"Those darn nosebleeds. They get worse around this time of year."

The weather can't decide between summer or fall. And the stress of being in Pandora again on top of the worsening headaches don't help.

"I remember you getting them bad." He hooks his thumbs on his pants pockets and shrugs, looking downright mouthwatering.

"Scared me shitless when the bleeding wouldn't stop no matter how much pressure you held."

"Until your mother mentioned stuffing tampons up my nose," I offer. "She's a good person. I miss her."

I cradle the basket to my chest.

"I should go. I made the mistake of getting ice cream first. Goodbye, Reed."

He doesn't step aside to let me by his imposing size. Did he get taller since the last time I saw him seven years ago? I walk around him, avoiding touching him, but the aisle is tight, and our arms graze.

Warm skin. Hard muscles. Reed's arms wrapped tight around me. His soft mouth on mine, our warm breaths intermingling. Rain pounding the ground below as we made love in his old treehouse on his parents' farm. Our first time and not our last.

Reed making love to me languidly.

Reed fucking me hard and fast.

Electric awareness zings up and down my spine. The place between my legs tingles and throbs.

I stammer, "I-I'm sorry," and rush to the cash register.

It's been too long since I've been with a guy. That's why my body reacts strongly to Reed's. Yes, that's it.

I pay for my groceries and carry them out to my car parked in front of the post office in the same parking lot, unsure of how many packages there is and in what sizes. I walk inside the post office and hope my experience—minus my embarrassing, but intense run-in with Reed—mirrors the positive experience I had at the grocery store.

The gal at the cash register looked to be my age. She didn't step back when she saw me. A hurtful reaction I endured from other girls growing up. There wasn't an ounce of recognition on her face. I didn't recognize her, either. She must be new. New blood in Pandora is good.

I head for the front counter.

"Good morning, Ms. Holton."

Eileen Holton is a widow my grandfather's age, seventy-five, with gleaming snow-white hair and glassy hazel eyes that can pierce or shine depending on her mood.

"Emersyn Collins." Her gaze is piercing.

She hasn't forgiven my grandfather for taking a shot at her grandson.

"When did you step foot in town?"

"Last night, ma'am." I respect my elders no matter how mean or hurtful their words can be.

The words I overheard her saying to my grandfather when he went to check on Granger in the hospital were downright horrible.

The bell over the door chimes. I don't look behind me to see who has come into the post office. I want out of here before I make a scene reaming this woman out for holding a grudge against a nice man like my grandfather. And the bullet from my grandfather's shotgun *grazed* Granger's thigh. A flesh wound, thank the stars.

"Can I have the packages for my grandfather, please? He said it's been a few days since he stopped by."

"It's been more than that. Tell him a week and a half is too long. And with his habit of ordering too much stuff, too." She shakes her head in disapproval.

"My apologies." I cringe.

This mean woman doesn't deserve apologies, but I would like to leave Pandora knowing things are better and not worse for my grandfather. Catching flies—or a gnat like Eileen—is best done with syrupy sweetness.

"My grandfather was in the nursing home recovering and going through rehab. He must have forgotten to contact you. Can I have his mail now? I have ice cream in my car."

She clucks her tongue and tips her head at the person behind me.

"Granger, get Mason Collins' packages."

"Yes, ma'am."

I face Reed's best friend. Granger Holton is older but not any less sexy than when he was eighteen. Six-foot-one. Tousled brown hair. Piercing hazel eyes. Five-o'clock shadow. A heart of gold beneath the muscles lining his body. He gives me a slight nod.

"Emersyn."

I don't say a word to him until he loads the last of Grandfather's packages in my car. Grandfather had so many, Granger had to bring them out on a hand truck. What the heck is he stocking up on?

"I'm sorry about your mother, Granger. My

grandfather said she lost her battle to brain cancer. Is that why you moved back? To help your grandmother run the business?"

Granger left Pandora and moved to Winston, a city two hours from Pendleton, soon after Reed headed for California.

"Yeah, I missed home. Missed the small town atmosphere. Living in a big city isn't what it's cracked up to be."

"My grandfather said you became a cop. That's great, Granger."

"Best thing to happen to me while I was there. Gave me the opportunity to take on a position as sheriff here."

His words are slow and thoughtful. I don't miss the anger and regret in his eyes. What happened to him in Winston? Granger is a good guy, even-keel and easy-going. "The more things change, the more they stay the same" doesn't ring true for Granger. Where did the sparkle in his eyes go?

"How many of you are there now?" I cross my arms and rest against the trunk.

"Over two dozen."

"What?! When I left, there were a handful."

He sighs. "Pandora's growing, Em. If you drive farther down, you'll see new neighborhoods and businesses going up left and right. It's the inevitable signs of change." He shrugs. "Em, there's something I have to tell you. Something I've been holding onto."

He sticks his hands in his pockets and pulls his shoulders inward. I brace myself. Reed has a similar pose when he's ready to drop the proverbial bomb.

"It's killing me inside. I…" He blows out a breath and looks me in the eye. "Remember the night your grandfather shot at me?"

"A mistake. He went to apologize, but your grandmother turned him away. He was angry at what they said. That my incestuous," — I detest that word — "genetics had gotten the better of me. He's a good man, Granger. Angry people do things that are not them."

I'm rambling. Sticking up for my grandfather. I love him so much.

"That's not what has me hurting, Emersyn."

He stares at the ground. Looks up. Remorse on his face.

"I didn't deliver your letter to Reed before he left. It got soaked in the downpour. I was with Amelia. She broke up with me over what you did to Reed's mom. I'm sorry."

He pulls me into his arms and crushes me against his chest, catching me off guard.

"I let you down, Em."

Throat clearing behind us. I untangle from Granger's hold and come face-to-face with Reed. His blue eyes blaze anger.

"Am I missing something? Is there something I should know?" His gaze shoots from me to Granger. "You messing with my girl?"

I glare back.

"Nothing's going on. I had something to tell Emersyn, that's all."

That's all??? What Granger told me is *monumental*. No wonder Reed felt the need to tell me he was ending our engagement seven years later. He never got my message.

Exhausted from the weight of our history with one another, I say in my most steady voice, "Goodbye again, Reed. Thanks for your help, Granger."

Then I book it out of there.

Granger and Reed are big boys. They can deal with Reed's misunderstanding of the situation like the decent and level-headed men they are.

6
REED

"You shouldn't be holding her like that." I yank on the boxing gloves and pound on the dummy's torso. "She's taken."

Punch. Bam. Pow. I'm changing this dude's name from Lifeless to Andy.

"What do you mean 'taken'?" Granger leans against the workbench. We're in the garage. The doors are open, letting in warm air.

"Engaged. Soon to be married," I spell out for him.

"I didn't see no ring."

Come to think of it, Granger's onto something. I was too busy staring at Emersyn's face to give a care what could be on her ring finger.

God, she's pretty.

Dark, arched brows. Long-as-fuck wild lashes. Pouty mouth. Gleaming white, straight teeth with a gap between the two front ones. Deep green eyes I could stare down into or look up at for hours.

Thick, chocolate-brown hair heavy in my hands as she rode my dick, hard. Or my fingers tangled in the silky strands as I thrust inside her until she came with a soft sigh that had me falling harder for her.

A large hand waves in front of my face. I blink. Scowl.

"Wipe that damn smirk off your face."

Granger's smirk widens. "You still have it bad for her. Grab at your chance. Once your suspension is over, it'll be non-stop ball for the next two months without a breather."

Punch. Bam. Pow. I need to get me one or more of these guys for my place.

"You need a breather to sort through whatever shit fucked up the two of you. Talk through it and clear the air. That's the only way you two can move on."

I pound the shit out of the dummy. "Philosophical mouthing-off from a guy that should take his own advice. What the hell happened in Winston? Why did you turn in your badge?"

There's more to Granger moving back other than

to help his grandmother run the post office after his mother's death six months ago.

"I thought you enjoyed being a city cop. And your cousin is more than capable and willing to help your grandmother."

Granger has made it clear being a sheriff is more his cup of tea.

"Nothing happened. Drop it already. I got tired of city living."

His standby line. Fine. His business. His damn life. But when Granger's ready to talk, I'll be there for him.

"What were you and Emers catching up on?"

"Stuff. I ruined something of hers. Was telling her how sorry I am for letting her down. I lost my shit and hugged her." He shrugs. "We good?"

"Yeah." I raise my glove. We fist-bump.

"Were you serious? Emersyn's engaged?"

I remove my gloves. "Yeah. I overheard her talking to him at the store. His name's Andy."

"Ah, shit, I'm sorry, Reed."

I toss the gloves onto the workbench.

"I'm not sorry or broken over it. She's a grown woman and has every right to move on with her life. To choose the man she wants to spend the rest of her life with."

"That's not what I'm hearing. I'm hearing the opposite. Don't regret not taking the chance to tell her what you did for her, Reed. Tell her how you paid for her education in the guise of grants and scholarships."

"She'll be pissed. She has pride. Is independent as fuck."

"Or she'll be grateful you kept your word and took care of her. Tell her. You owe her that after what you said to her at your mom's funeral. Emersyn needs to know you care. Cared so much you kept your promise. Do me a solid, and fucking tell her, okay?"

"If I don't want to?"

He jabs his finger into my chest.

"She's my friend. You're my friend, too. Do right by the two of you, of your memories together. Your promise to her is what got you to fight harder for your place in the Majors."

I knock his finger off my chest. "She shoved my mom off a cliff."

"An accident. It was pouring buckets. The ground was wet. Your mom slipped and fell off."

"So you're telling me Emersyn lied?" I trench my fingers in my hair and pull at the strands.

Granger sighs. "I don't know, Reed. Just talk to her."

"And if she tells the same story? That she and my mom fought over Emersyn seeing me, then what?"

"Your choice. Walk away or forgive her."

7

EMERSYN

Though the floor fan is at full blast, it's sweltering hot inside the bedroom. And my head is pounding. I also miss Charlie like crazy. But Grandpa loves having him at the house.

How could I refuse Charlie staying there when they're happy as clams in each other's company? Not to mention Grandpa promised to follow the instructions for taking care of his new hip to the T.

My grandfather... He's making my time in Pandora easy, and I made life a living hell for him when he took me in rather than put me up for foster care when my mom abandoned me.

I stare at the ceiling, wide awake with my arm slung across my forehead. If I can't make life better for him by mending the rifts, I'll convince him to return with me to Pendleton.

But he's stubborn and will insist he stays put. Pandora will be his final resting place, I'm certain of it.

My headache worsens. The air from the fan isn't cutting through the dry heat. I toss off the covers and pad to the kitchen. I remember seeing an ice pack in the freezer.

I swaddle it with a dishrag, and too tired and grouchy to care whether Reed could be up, I head out the door and plop down on the top step of the front porch.

I hold the ice to my temple. Cold seeps into my skin and calms the aching throb. Smiling, I lean back, prop myself up with one arm on the cement, and close my eyes.

"Better. So much better."

I bite down on my bottom lip. Hum low in my throat when a breeze coasts over my face and cools my hot skin.

"What I wouldn't give for a cold-ass beer."

"Come over and you can have the last IPA."

Reed. My eyes flare open. He zones in on my nose and tries for a straight face but can't. He laughs. I yank the tampon from my nose and hurl the bloody mess at him. He dodges it with lightning speed.

"Not funny, Reed Haider. Nosebleeds are a pain in the butt."

"I'm sorry." He picks up the tampon on the non-bloody side and drops it in the garbage can. "But you know I can't *not laugh* when you have one of those suckers in."

"It's not a sucker. It's a soaker."

"Sucker. Soaker. To-mae-toe, to-ma-toe."

"Really?" A smile stretches across my face.

I love hearing the teasing lilt in Reed's voice.

Needing to see more of him, I sit forward with my elbows on my knees and my chin resting in my palms; the ice pressed against my temple.

Shirtless. Loose-fitting pajama pants hanging low on his hips. Bare feet. Tall. Lean. Sinfully hot. Mouthwatering. I move the ice pack from my temple to my cheek. Right then left. I'm burning up from the inside out with how much I want to jump his bones.

"Why are you up, Emersyn?" Low. Husky. Velvety soft.

"Not sleeping well. Too hot." I put down the ice pack and fan my face. Boy, is he ever smoking hot. "Small bed."

"There's a spare bedroom with a king-size bed. You can spread out to your heart's content."

Goodness, did he just say what I think he said? A mental image of me naked on the king bed with his face buried between my legs flare bright in my mind. I fan my toasty cheeks with both hands.

"You okay?" Knowing gleam in his eyes, the light from his driveway shining bright in the night.

"I'm fine. I can't go with you, Reed."

"Even for a *cold-ass* beer?"

"No."

"I have chocolate cream pie in the fridge."

My favorite. His favorite.

"Remember me eating pie off your body, Emers?"

A dollop of chocolate on one nipple. A dollop of whipped cream on the other. Chocolate smeared between my breasts, on my belly, and above my bikini line. Reed's tongue lapping off the chocolate. His mouth sucking the cream off. I groan. Clamp my knees together.

Reed grasps his bottom lip between his teeth, as though holding in a moan. He stares at my mouth.

"Come home with me, Emersyn Collins." Sultry. Hot need in his voice.

I shake my head, too turned on to speak.

"Because you're happy with someone named Andy?"

He scowls.

My eyes must be wide.

"Your conversation from the store. I'm sorry. I shouldn't have listened in. My just due." He crosses his arms and kicks at the ground. "What I felt…" He blows out a breath. "What I overheard tore me up, Emers."

He was jealous? I don't know what to make of his confession, but I can tell the truth. This truth won't destroy him.

"Andy is a girl. She's my best friend, and yes, I'm happy with her, but I'm definitely into guys."

Translation: I'm into you, and I'm willing to go home with you.

I cover my flaming face. Oh, God.

"Emers. Babe."

The tenderness in his voice, the desire beneath the tenderness… I remove my hands from my face.

"Us alone isn't a good idea. Not when you have chocolate pie nearby."

He chuckles and swipes his palm over his dark hair, tousled and unruly from sleep.

"I get it."

And I can't stop staring. Wide shoulders. Broad

chest. Dark patch of hair. Sinful strip disappearing inside his PJ bottoms. Those six-pack abs. I groan. Why does he have to look so stinking sexy?

"Well, okay, good night, Emers. I'll be thinking of you when I sleep like a baby with the a/c going."

"What?!" I shoot to my feet. "You big shit, why didn't you say so sooner?"

I hop off the steps and follow him to his place, then realize I forgot something.

"I should grab a tampon or two."

"No need. I have a box. Bought it after you left the store. It's good to have a spare."

"Reed."

Emotion overcomes me. I throw my arms around his neck, and on the tips of my toes, I drop a kiss on his cheek.

"Thank you," I murmur over his warm skin.

His arm curves across my lower back, and I'm pulled flush against his body.

Soft cotton brushes my bare legs. His pelvis presses against mine, the bulge under his PJ bottoms very noticeable. My sleep shorts are flimsy.

His pecs and chest hair caress my breasts through my tank top. My nipples harden. Heat pools between my legs. I cradle the back of his head in my palms and arch against him, needing to be as close as possible.

"Emers, Jesus, you feel so fucking good, babe." His groan reverberates against my chest.

My breasts and my sex ache and throb with need.

"Reed. Please."

He crushes his mouth on mine, and I cling to him. To his body. To his mouth. Tasting him. Sweet like honey. Touching my tongue on his. Warm and wet. I skim my hands down the cords of muscles on his arms. Flatten my palms over his pecs. Tunnel my fingers in his chest hair.

Coarse. Soft. I can't decide. He just feels so darn good beneath my fingers.

I trail my fingertips low, lower, until I'm coasting them over the ridges of his abs. He breaks off our kiss.

"Emers."

He's out of breath. Good. So am I.

"Inside your place, now." My heart beats loud and fast in my ears.

"We can't go back, Em."

"We can. One night. Make me yours for one night, Reed."

"Afterward?"

I nip on his bottom lip. Suck its fullness into my mouth. Run the tip of my tongue over the seams.

"Are we still talking?"

He clasps my head in his palms and looks me dead-set in the eyes. "If we do this, no regrets?"

"None."

He kisses me, robbing me of breath and resolve. My chest aches. One night won't be enough.

We come up for air.

"The women from last night, we won't be in the same bed you—"

He does the nipping this time, making love to my bottom lip with his teeth and his tongue.

"Nothing happened. The women are fans. They won a contest to help bake my signature pecan pie. When I saw the hurt in your eyes…"

He drops kisses on my forehead, my nose, my lips.

"I had Granger drop them off at their hotel. I'm sorry for my hurtful words, Emers."

His apology and me smoothing over his misunderstanding that Andy is my BFF and not my boyfriend, shift whatever was off-kilter between us. We're on the same footing again.

I cradle his face in my palm. "Thank you for the

apology. I accept. Thank you for what you said about the women. I appreciate your honesty."

"I've kept nothing from you, Emersyn."

But I've withheld truths from him. Damning truths. Do I continue to protect him from his mother's god-awful secrets and lies? Or do I tell him, hoping to God, he'll give me back the most important piece of me I left behind—my heart.

"Ready, Emers?"

He hoists me up. I wrap my legs around his waist.

"I'm ready."

8
REED

I set her down in front of my bed. Tuck strands of hair behind her ear. Cup her face in my palm.

"I missed you."

"Don't say that, Reed."

Agony in her voice, and her green eyes shimmer. She circles her arms around my neck and pulls me down with her onto the bed. I keep my weight off her with my arms resting alongside her head.

"It's the truth." I search her face for signs of regret.

If she doesn't want to be with me, I'll walk her next door with regret a dull ache in my chest for not contacting her sooner. Seven years. Why the fuck did I wait so long to claim what has always been mine—Emersyn's heart?

She turns away from me. I gently nudge her chin with my knuckle until our gazes meet.

"If you don't want to take this further, I'm fine with just holding you."

She bites down on her lower lip. "It's not that. What you said makes me want things I can't have."

"Like what?" I skim my finger along the graceful arch of her cheek and down her jawline. "What do you want most, Emersyn?"

I grasp her chin between my fingers, ready to move Heaven and Earth for her.

"You. I want you, Reed. Our history together… You know and understand me better than anyone ever has."

Her voice trembles. She blinks back her tears. I can't stop staring at the earnestness in her eyes. This woman… She undoes me with her emotion-filled words.

"You still carry feelings for me?"

Jesus Christ, I'm a cocky bastard for believing such nonsense.

"Yes," she says so softly I almost missed that one important word. "You have my heart, Reed. I miss you, too."

I groan. Kiss her thoroughly. We're a mish-mash of tongues and teeth.

"I need you, Reed. Want you inside me. Have dreamt of you constantly."

"I want you, too. Have also had my fair share of wet dreams about you."

"Reed."

She grabs onto my shoulders and kneads the muscles. Wraps her slender legs around my waist. Grinds her pelvis on mine and digs the balls of her heels into my ass cheeks.

"Sweetheart." I'm panting. My cock pushes against the front of my pants. "We need to get our clothes the fuck off."

"Yes, right." She covers her eyes with her arm. Laughs. Low. Sultry.

She's sexy with that crooked smile on her face.

I untangle her legs from around my waist, hop off the bed, and strip. She yanks her tank top over her head and shimmies out of her shorts and panties.

I'm dizzy with how sexy she is stripped bare with her arms outstretched and her legs open, ready for me.

I glove my erection and take my time getting on the bed.

I want to look my fill.

I miss seeing her naked.

I was right. Same girl. Different body. Not a girl anymore. Emersyn is all woman.

Big, round tits. Dark areolas. Flat abs. Roundness to her hips. Wide hips made for making babies. But I'm thinking ahead of myself.

I get on the bed and drag my nose from her hair to her navel, stopping along the way to worship her with my mouth and my tongue.

I nuzzle her neck and suck and lick at the sensitive spot below her right ear. She digs her fingernails into my shoulders. I lavish attention on her tits next using my mouth and my fingers, tasting and tweaking the little balls. She moans and moves her head side to side. Smiling with satisfaction, I go low and drop kisses on her stomach and blow at the wetness I left behind. She squirms and pushes at my head, demanding I go down on her. Emersyn isn't the shy girl I remember making love to. This woman is a hellcat, and I'm loving it.

I suck on her clit. Mouth her wet pussy. Lick and lap up her flavor. Her hips buck off the bed. I hook my arms around her thighs and drag my nose across her inner thigh before I go in for another taste.

"Reed."

Small fingers grab at my hair and tug.

"Please, Reed. I need you inside me."

I move up until my thickness fills the hot place between her legs.

"No regrets, Emersyn."

"None."

I slide my erection inside her tight, wet channel inch by inch.

"One night, Reed." She shakes her head. "Our agreement."

Is that so?

I thrust in and out of her.

She pulls back her knees. I thrust again, balls deep inside her.

"Reconsider," I edge out through my teeth, trying to hang on for dear life. Fuck, I can't come. Not yet. But hell, I'm so close.

She laughs. My cock hardens more if that's possible. Jesus, her throaty laughter…

"Not fair when you're making me feel so darn good, Six."

"I miss you, One." I kiss her between her beautiful green eyes. Kiss the tip of her nose. "I miss how your eyes darken when you're turned on. Miss the sexy way your mouth parts when you're ready to come. Miss your soft sigh when you do. I fucking miss you, Emers."

"Not fair, Reed. So not fair." Tears in her eyes.

I intertwine our fingers. Place our hands above her head. Move in and out of her. Slow. Deliberately slow. I need her to know how much I want her and what she means to me.

Emersyn closes her eyes. Smiles that crooked smile of hers.

"I reconsider."

Satisfaction courses through me, and I thrust faster. Deeper. Harder.

"Oh my God, Reed. I… Now. Oh, God. Now."

Her mouth parts. She sighs. I pound into her. I'm dizzy. Out of my mind crazy for this woman. I'm wound tight from my balls to the head of my cock. I go harder. Her inner muscles clench my throbbing dick. The pressure eases. Eases more. Heat envelopes my body.

"Fuck. Oh, fuck." I come, hard.

Out of breath, I loosen my grip on her small fingers and glance down. Emersyn stares up at me with a lopsided smile. I run my knuckle over her flushed skin. Smooth my mouth over hers.

"Thank you for reconsidering, Em. You won't regret it."

Then why the hell did she have tears in her eyes when I returned to bed after discarding the condom in the bathroom?

9

EMERSYN

I'm at the rental for my laptop when someone pulls in next to my car and parks. I recognize Andy's Jeep.

Squealing with excitement, I run over and wrap my arms around a smiling Andy.

"Holy cow, girly, you are a sight for sore eyes." I put her at arm's length. "But what are you doing here? Don't you have to supervise at the Allen wedding?"

"*Two days* away."

Translation: she'll be here one day, tops.

"Elle and Harper are wonderful. You did good hiring them, Em. They take initiative. Makes working with them enjoyable with how detailed they are."

I pout. "I'm jealous. You never say those awesome words about me."

"Initiative? Wonderful?"

"Enjoyable. Detailed."

"But you are, Em. The clients rave like crazy."

"Really?" I loop my arm around hers. "How come you never told me?"

"It would go to your head and you would float off into the sky with how big your head would get."

"Ha-ha, not." I lead her inside the house. "No, seriously, why are you here? Don't get me wrong, I love the company, but life in a small town is," I shrug, "boring."

"Reed is here. I'll be your buffer." Andy covers her yawn with the back of her hand.

I steer her to the kitchen and make her a cup of coffee. "You mean my wingman?"

"No, silly. Buffer. Barrier. The one that'll stop you from doing or saying stuff that you'll later regret."

Two thoughts cross my mind. One, Andy can never know I slept with Reed. I'll never hear the last of it, that I should have made him work harder for his second chance with me. But... Two, I *slept* with Reed. We made love. Snuggled in bed. Fell asleep together. Woke up together.

Something we never did, spend a night falling

asleep in each other's arms. We were afraid of getting caught.

"Like what?" I finally say. I pour myself a cup of coffee, too.

"Telling him you miss him. That you cry on the anniversary of the day he proposed to you. Kissing him. Getting tangled in the sheets with him. Shit like that. Romantic, Em."

He asked for more than one night.

I agreed.

Oh, God, *I agreed*.

I sip my coffee. "Not romantic but tragic. First crushes don't last. It's also been seven years, Andy. We've changed."

Were my tears last night of happiness or sadness? Being with him again, I felt both, unable to separate one from the other when I thought over whether Reed and I could have a future together.

She sets her hand on mine. "Tell him, Emersyn. Get everything off your chest. That's the only way you'll move on."

"And how well did that advice work for me with Scott? I told him how I felt. Let him know I needed more affection and intimacy. Guess what he did?"

I never told this part to Andy.

"He got tired of me asking. I found him bending his secretary over his desk doing her doggy style."

I told Andy Scott cheated, but I didn't go into details.

Andy stands and has the nerve to mime "doggy style," thrusting her hips and smacking at the air with her palm. She looks ridiculous. I sputter laughter. She laughs, too. We finish our coffees in silence.

"Where's Charlie?" She rinses our mugs and puts them in the dishwasher.

"With my grandfather. He misses Red."

"Poor guy."

"Hey, Charlie is a very well-behaved pup. He won't give my grandfather trouble. My grandfather is lucky to have him there."

"I meant your granddad, Em. That's nice of you to share Charlie. Missing someone is hard."

Her voice catches. My poor friend. She misses her sister.

"I can't wait to meet the old bugger." She smiles, composing herself. Andy recovers her emotions in the blink of an eye.

"He's hilarious cracking jokes with a straight face. And his laughter… He has one of those laughs you can't help but join in on. I see why you love him so much."

"Let's have you two meet in person." I text my grandfather the plan.

I don't want to surprise him.

He has a weak heart and didn't tell me until this morning. I jumped out of bed and ran over to his place again, rushing out of the bedroom with a hurried, "I'll see you later," to a very naked, but sleepy Reed Haider, as I yanked on my clothes.

Grandfather had a heart attack after his hip surgery. Thank the stars he had it while still in the hospital.

That stubborn man.

I lectured him good for not having the hospital staff call me. I would have been there ASAP.

"Do you have errands to run today?"

"Are you volunteering to be my buffer with the townspeople?" I haven't gone into the heart of Pandora yet.

"Caught."

I hug her. "Thank you for being a great friend. No errands, but I would like to clean up my grandfather's property and get it ready for fall and winter."

I let go of her and grab my bag off the kitchen counter.

"I also plan on doing more work. That's why I stopped by. For my laptop."

She picks up the laptop, cord, and wireless mouse off the coffee table and holds everything to her chest. "Got it. I'll help at your grandfather's."

"You'll collect eggs from the henhouse, mow my grandfather's overgrown lawn, and pick vegetables from the garden for spaghetti made from scratch?"

"Why not? In my past life I was a farm girl."

I roll my eyes. We head out. Just as I'm locking the door, I hear the rumble of a big truck. The lifted red pickup truck with the monster tires parks alongside Reed's truck.

The door to Reed's place opens. The truck's driver-side door opens and shut. Two things happen. Reed glances my way and shoots me this look that promises more hot nights in his arms as the a/c cools our bodies before, during, and after sweaty AF sex.

My insides quiver. So does the place between my legs. I'm staring so hard at Reed, I don't register Andy's gasp and my laptop hitting the ground until Andy's nails dig into my arm.

"Who is that?" she says, breathless-like.

"Andy, I'm disappointed," I tease, unable to tear my gaze away from Reed's blinding smile. "As a fanatic baseball fan, you should be able to pick him out of a lineup."

"No, Em, the guy with him."

"Granger? He's Reed's best friend."

"Granger." She says his name slowly as though testing whether she's saying his name correctly. "Are you certain that's his name?"

"One hundred percent." I face her. Her skin is the color of her white denim shorts, her paleness made more obvious by her sapphire-blue tank top. "Andy, are you okay?"

"Yes. Yes, I'm fine."

She's not. She's breathing fast, her gaze fixed. She also has a death grip on my arm. She's panicking. Soon she'll hyperventilate. This happened twice in the five years I've known her — when her parents died and when they found her missing sister's skeletal remains.

I break into action. "Reed, do you have paper lunch bags?"

He nods, having run over at seeing how god-awful Andy looks.

"Get it. She's hyperventilating." I lower Andy to a sitting position on the porch.

Reed returns. I place the bag over Andy's nose and mouth.

"Slow breaths in through your nose and out your mouth." I rub her back.

Andy is smart. Perceptive. She'll understand what is happening to her body.

But why the fierce reaction to seeing Granger?

"You'll be okay. It'll be okay."

Holding onto the bag, she shakes her head and points at the dented laptop on the ground.

"Do you know how many times I've dropped that darn thing? *Countless*. Anyway, if it doesn't start up, I'll get another."

"Your work." Muffled words.

"In the cloud."

Muffled laughter. "Planned."

"I did. Just in case my laptop gets a virus or my best friend drops it."

She takes the bag away from her mouth. "I'm sorry, Em."

Her breathing is back to normal. Her color, too.

"It's not a big deal." I lean into her. "What happened?" I say in a quiet voice.

The guys are on my driveway watching us.

"Nothing, Em. It's nothing." Her gaze zones in on Granger. He locks his eyes on Andy.

I don't understand what the hell is going on between them, but I have manners. I take Andy's hand, help her to her feet, and make the introductions.

"Reed, Granger, this is my best friend, Andy. She drove from Pendleton to visit me and my grandfather."

"Nice to meet you," they say in unison.

"Do you live and work in Pendleton, Andy?" Granger asks, saying Andy's name slowly as though testing if her name fits her.

What the heck?

"Where I prefer to spend my time."

"How about Winston? You spend time in Winston?"

"Not at all. The city's dirty."

There's an edge to Andy's voice. There's a hard glint in Granger's eyes. What is going on with these two? Reed and I exchange a "look."

"Would you two like to get a room?" Reed asks.

I give him the stink-eye. That butt.

Andy tips her chin. "No, thanks."

"Hell, no." Granger stomps to his truck.

Andy looks after him then gets in her Jeep. The door slams shut.

"And I thought we have issues," I say.

"They definitely have history." He tips his head at Andy's Jeep. "You two headed to your grandfather's?"

I nod and share with Reed Grandpa's heart attack. "If something happens to him while he's under my watch…"

My voice trembles.

"Hey, it'll be okay."

I'm pulled into his muscular arms and cradled against his wide shoulder with his big palm on the back of my head.

"He's strong, Emers. He always has been."

"There's so much to do, and I don't want him lifting a finger." What I told Andy is a quarter of the work that needs to get done before the weather turns.

"Tell me."

I do.

"How about Granger and I do the heavy lifting? Unless you or Andy mind. You ladies look strong as fuck and can probably whoop our asses."

Reed flexes his arm and shows off his bulging bicep. I smile. He's adorable and sexy, a juxtaposition of the boy I fell in love with and the man I'm falling hard for, again.

"I don't mind, Reed. I'm all in for a man doing his fair share." I give the side of his face a solid pat.

His eyes sparkle. "Meet you there?"

"Sure." I glance at my dented laptop lying on the ground.

Reed looks where I'm looking.

"I have a computer I'm willing to share. For a price." He waggles his brows.

"I would love to, but Andy needs me."

He pulls me back into the warmth of his solid body.

"You're a good friend, Emersyn Collins."

"I wasn't. I let you down, Reed."

With my lies.

With how scared I was that night.

I should have fought harder for what we had, but I was *so* scared.

"We should talk." He puts me at arm's length. "The serious kind. About what happened that night."

Pleading in his eyes.

My heart pounds out of control.

My mouth is dry.

"I'm not ready. I'm sorry."

I'm not ready.

I'm sorry.

I care for you.

So much.

I care so much, I'm not ready to tell him the god-awful truth. My lies and secrets have the power to *destroy* him and our chance for happiness again.

"I don't want to pressure you, but I leave Sunday."

"I'll think on it."

"Thank you, Em."

Three days. I have three days to make a life-changing decision.

10

EMERSYN

"Hey, doing okay over here?" Reed comes from behind and wraps me in his arms. "Need any help?"

I'm at the sink washing my hands after cutting up vegetables from the garden for a salad. We're at my grandfather's, ready to sit down for a home-cooked meal after having worked tirelessly on his property.

"You can play referee to the stewing, hormonal teenagers in the corner." I tip my head at Andy and Granger.

They're on opposite ends of the small dining table setting out silverware and drinking glasses. The entire time here, they've been circling one another like the sun circles the earth, never touching, but burning hot one minute and cold the next.

"What is going on with them?" I dry my hands on a dishrag.

"I'm as boggled as you are." He tilts my face to his and kisses me square on the mouth.

Soft.

Mouth-on-mouth.

Bitter beer.

Sweaty. Salty.

I want more.

I open for him.

Whimper when he deepens the kiss.

He kisses me so thoroughly, my toes curl.

As though from a distance, I hear someone clearing their throat. I break off the kiss, hot from embarrassment over our PDA.

"Reed." My eyes flutter open.

"It's okay, babe." He tucks me into his body, resting his chin on the top of my head. "We're showing the randy, temperamental teenagers how it's done."

He says it loud enough for Andy and Granger to hear. Grandpa is out of ear-shot. He's sitting in the living room in his favorite recliner with Charlie at his feet chewing on a dog toy.

I stare forward and catch our reflection in the window.

I can get used to the comforting way Reed holds me tight in his arms. Or the tender way he looks at me when I talk of my life at college and my life post-college with Charlie, Andy, and my friends. We snuggled and talked into the early hours of morning after we made love.

I can also get used to the hardening of his jaw and the anger bright in his eyes when I told him of my wreck-of-a-relationship with Scott, including how Scott cheated on me.

But I don't know if I can stay in Reed's life, see him every day, and not be reminded of the secrets and lies I carry deep inside for the sake of protecting him and preserving his mother's clean and wholesome image.

Charlotte Haider was smart, kind, funny, a loving mother, and an attentive wife. She was a woman from old money, Reed's dad meeting her at college. With her bright smile and sparkling blue eyes, she could do no wrong. But she did. Lies, secrets, and betrayal.

A knock at the door.

I blink.

Reed nips on my ear. "Here's to playing referee to

another couple that needs to either duke it out in the boxing ring or get tangled in the sheets."

"My grandfather would kick butt, and, ew."

I untangle from Reed's arms and hurry to the door, beating my grandfather to it. No way will I let him ruin my attempt at smoothing over his rift with our guest before she has the chance to cross over the threshold.

I open the door. "Ms. Holton. Nice of you to make it." I sweep out my arm for her to come inside.

"Call me Eileen, Emersyn."

"Thank you." I close the door. I was wrong to worry. My grandfather hasn't gotten up from his stubborn position in his recliner.

"Grandfather, would you like to come over and say 'hi' to Eileen?" I meet my grandfather's eyes. Shoot my brows low. Tip my head slightly Eileen's way.

"It's okay, Emersyn." She pats my arm. "Hip surgery can be exhausting. I had mine replaced last year. You stay put, Mason." She hands me a bottle of Cabernet Sauvignon. "I had one of these in the cellar. Pairs well with tomato sauce."

"Thank you." I take the bottle from her. "Grandpa, Eileen brought you a gift."

Her eyes widen with panic. "The wine's for everyone."

"Sure, Eileen. We all know you brought the bottle to hit me over the head with."

Collective gasps.

"Now, you listen here, Mason Collins."

She marches toward my grandfather. Grandfather rises. Granger steps between them and sets his big paws on his grandmother's arms.

"Grandma, forgive, already. You two are heading closer to the eighth decade of your life. Life's too short to be holding grudges."

"Well, when said that way…" Eileen wriggles out of Granger's hold and nudges him to the side. She tips her chin at my grandfather. "My apologies, Mason. I hope from now forward, we can be civil."

She futzes with her hair and tugs down her shirt. Her white hair gleams in the light, and the shirt's material stretches across her chest. Grandpa stares, and I see why.

Eileen is a pretty lady.

He clears his throat. Mumbles, "Apology accepted. I'm sorry for what I said earlier. Thank you for the wine. Very thoughtful of you."

Wow.

He walks over, clasps her hand then mine. "Shall we eat?"

Andy, me, and the guys nod, speechless at what just went down.

"Will you say grace?" He looks at Eileen with something close to tenderness.

The surprises keep on coming. I suck in a breath and catch Reed's attention with my eyes. I tip my head at the couple once, twice, wanting to mouth, "They have history, too."

Andy also thinks so. She eyes them. Glances at Granger. Swivels her keen observation to Reed and me. I'm waiting for her head to do a three-sixty spin on her shoulders. My hand firmly in my grandfather's, I motion for her with my head to sit in the empty seat next to Granger. She shakes her head. I glower. She shakes her head, again.

I'm ready to lay down the smack-down when Reed saves us from seeing two grown women putting one another in a head-lock, offering his chair to Andy.

I swear Granger sighs in relief.

Those two.

Eileen laughs at something my grandfather whispered in her ear. My eyes widen at how comfortable and relax they look with one another.

I shake my head.

These two.

"Ready for grace?" Grandfather asks.

Collective nods and the four of us mind our manners and let our elders sit before we take our seats.

"Everyone hold hands," Eileen reminds us.

I set my hands in Granger's and my grandfather's and duck my head. Eileen says grace. I sneak a peek at Reed sitting across from me. He's seated between Granger and Andy.

He smiles. I smile back. He's such a good guy, and I don't need three days to decide.

May he someday forgive me for deciding to keep his mom's secrets from him.

"Amen."

"Amen." I let go of Granger's hand and my grandfather's. Let go of the hope that Reed and I could have a life together.

I'll continue to protect him.

I'll preserve his mother's clean image.

I won't let her betrayal stain her clean image.

Reed remembers her as a woman that could do no wrong. I love him so much I don't want to destroy his memories of her.

Oh, God.
Oh, God.
I love him.
I love Reed Haider.

11

EMERSYN

The next day is a hot mess.

Andy bolts before I have the chance to make coffee and slyly ask her about Granger. Her text wakes me from my dream of Reed slathering me with chocolate cream pie.

Ping. Ping. Ping.

Sassy: I'm sorry for leaving. Will make it up to you

Sassy: I'll wear the ape suit at Chloe's bridal shower

Sassy: I can kick Scott in the balls for u too

My friend is conflicted. Remorseful in one message. Too accommodating with her second message. Vindictive in the third.

I call her, but my call goes straight to voicemail.

She must be driving. I text her then realize Andy needs to stay focused. On. The. Road.

I toss my cell on the nightstand next to the bed.

Ping.

Andy?

I grab for my phone. It's a message from Reed.

Hot stuff: Run over to your granddad's with u?

Me: You sure?

Hot stuff: Afraid I can't keep up?

Me: Worried you'll trip over your feet and hurt yourself when I shoot you my blinding smile

Hot stuff: LOL

Another message pops up on my screen.

Stubborn: Em, I hate to be a bother, but can you come over, NOW

Not good when my grandfather texts in caps.

I call him.

"Did something happen? Is Charlie okay? Did my lovebug make a mess on your floor? He hasn't had an accident since he was ten-months old, Grandpa."

"Em." Deep sigh. "It's not Charlie. He's fine. He's the one that found the chicken."

"Chicken? We had spaghetti." Charlie begged for table scraps last night. I reminded Grandpa in a firm, but gentle voice, I've banned Charlie Brown from having human food.

My phone pings.

"Look at your screen."

I look.

He sent a photo of a chicken with its head cut off and a piece of paper stuck to its chest with a screwdriver.

Bile rises in my throat. My stomach drops like it does on roller-coaster rides. I cover my mouth. Shake my head when I see what is written on the paper.

"Sin begets sin. Filth doesn't belong in Pandora."

"Did you call the sheriff, Grandpa?"

His silence is my answer. My throat tightens. My grandfather refusing to call the sheriff is my fault. How can he face Reed's dad after my confession?

"Emersyn, you don't need to come by today, sweetheart. Charlie and I will be fine."

Defeat in his voice. He's fought my fight for so long, and I'm tired of it.

"I'll go into town and file a report." I put the call on speaker and hop out of bed. "I'll show them the picture you sent me. You rest up and let Charlie spoil you with his slobbery kisses."

I yank on my clothes.

"Grandpa, have you had trouble like this before?"

Thick silence.

"Sticks and stones may break my bones, but words can never hurt me," I remind him.

"Not since you left home, Emersyn."

His answer sucks air from my lungs. I can't get in a decent breath. My chest aches. My legs are rubbery. I lower myself onto the floor.

Why did I believe returning to Pandora was a good idea?

"I love you." I end the call and bawl.

12

EMERSYN

Reed insists he come with me as soon as he saw me in the driveway with tears in my eyes.

On the ride over, I tell him what happened. I don't tell him my grandfather didn't call it in.

"When I get a hold of the bastard that did that shit…" He clenches his jaw. His hold on my hand tightens.

I grimace. "Reed."

"I'm sorry, Emers." He loosens his hold and parks his truck in front of the sheriff's office.

Someone must have informed the office we were coming. Uniformed officers mill near the front door. There's also a large group of people in front of the mayor's office, watching us.

Great, my own welcoming party.

Reed cuts the engine, and I slide out of his truck. He walks over to me, and calm and collected, he takes my hand in his and faces his dad, a sheriff, and his grandfather, the retired mayor of Pandora.

"Dad. Gramps." He tips his head. "Emersyn is here to file a report on behalf of her grandfather. Someone left a headless chicken on his property for Emers' dog to find."

"Is that so?" His grandfather looks me up and down, seeming to assess my worth.

A tall, dark-haired woman pushes her way from the middle of the crowd and glares. "You're garbage, Emersyn Collins. Get the hell out of our town."

Libby Armstrong. She had a big crush on Reed senior year of high school. He turned down her aggressive advances.

People grumble and march forward as one. A mob. Reed tightens his hold. I slip my hand from his and distance myself. Not his fight. No one knew of our secret relationship except one man, and he has the most to lose if he acknowledges it. I won't cause a rift between Reed, his family, and the people of Pandora.

I fix my gaze on Reed's grandfather.

"I'm not here to cause trouble. I'm here to help my grandfather."

I shift my focus to Granger and his grandmother.

"My grandfather has said mean and hurtful words in my defense. He's also done things he shouldn't have done coming to my defense. He was in the wrong, but he's also in the right for what he said and did."

I address the group.

"My father's sin is not mine or my grandfather's. What my mom's half-brother did is the worst betrayal of trust and family."

I sweep my gaze over the crowd, forcing them to acknowledge how they've been treating me since my mother abandoned me at my grandfather's doorstep.

"I was conceived from rape, but I'm not the criminal. My mother's half-brother is. I'm not my father's victim. My mom was. She didn't ask to be violated and get pregnant. She didn't want me but my grandmother pressured her to keep me. I'm sad and sorry for her, but I'm not sorry she left me at my grandfather's."

I ball my hands at my sides and inhale a shaky breath.

"Stop treating me like I'm worthless and beneath you. Stop treating my grandfather like shit. He's a good man and has shown me nothing but love, kindness, and acceptance. He's better than all of you put together. Everyone carries secrets."

I glare at Reed's grandfather, the hurt and anger I've bottled up over the years spilling out.

"Everyone has betrayed someone's trust, me included. Stop judging and accept me as I am."

Reed's grandfather points a thick finger at me. "You have *no right* telling us what to do and how to think. You have *no right* being near my grandson. Your filth will *stain* him. Get out of town, Emersyn. We tolerated your freakishness long enough."

"My grandfather—"

"All will be forgiven if you leave town and never come back."

"I… You can't ask that of me." Tears burn the back of my eyes.

"Why should it matter? You haven't been back since you left."

"Please, he's getting older. He'll need my help."

"My grandmother and I will look out for him, Emers," Granger says with pity in his eyes. "We'll make sure he's well taken care of."

Alongside him, his grandmother is crying.

I nod, acknowledging the truth. Granger won't

risk his job for me. I don't expect him to. His family's history began and will end in Pandora.

"Emersyn." Reed reaches for me.

"Stay away from her, Reed," his father commands. "Did you forget she confessed to shoving your mom?"

"Do you stand by those words, Emersyn?"

He steps between me and his family. Pleads with his eyes for me to give him the truth from that night.

"Emers, please," he says in this soft voice.

"Reed." I sob harder. "I'm sorry."

He's shoved out of the way by his grandfather.

"She's guilty. Took too long to answer. You get on out of here. Get."

He pushes and pushes. I stumble back. Tears blur my vision and streak down my face. I swipe at them. Reed is standing between his dad and his grandfather. They have a firm grip on his shoulders. With his family is where he belongs.

My chest aching, I turn and run.

I don't make it out of the parking lot before there's commotion behind me. Are they coming after me? Were their words not enough, they have to hurt me physically, too? I glance over my shoulder, my heart rate picking up.

Reed's grandfather is on the ground. Granger is

doing chest compressions, and Reed is giving his grandfather mouth-to-mouth.

I sprint over.

"What happened?" I ask out of breath.

"He collapsed." Reed's dad grabs at his hair. He looks on with tears in his eyes. "We called nine-one-one."

Granger and Reed are doing everything right, but they're missing something. I rack my brain. Andy made us take CPR.

"Did he say or do anything before he collapsed?"

"He clutched at his chest." Eileen wrings her hands.

Bingo. "Is there a defibrillator in the station?"

"I'll get it." A deputy runs inside and returns with the AED.

I attach the pads, turn on the machine, and follow the instructions. Sirens blare closer in the tense silence as we stay clear of Elias Haider's body and wait for the defibrillator to deliver a shock.

It delivers the shock. Mr. Haider's eyes burst open, and he gasps. Relief floods through my body. If Reed had lost his grandfather… My stomach tightens at how devastated he and his father would be. The Haider men are close.

I lean in and for Mr. Haider only, I say my final words to him.

"Forgive me. I'm sorry. Sorry she died. Sorry I couldn't save her for you. Thank you for giving my grandfather another chance for a better life. I'll keep my promise if you keep yours."

He fumbles for my hand. The medics put an oxygen mask over his face. I get off my knees and watch them put him on a gurney and into the ambulance.

Reed and his father hurry to Reed's truck. He's forgotten about me. Understandable. Granger walks over. I shake my head and make the long walk back to the rental.

On my way out of the parking lot, no one cusses at me or calls me crude names. No one comes after me and yanks on my hair or pushes me to the ground from behind, taking me by surprise. There's nothing but silence.

I let the tears fall.

I did the right thing keeping the truth from them.

Elias and Charlotte's secrets, lies, and betrayals are not mine to tell.

13

EMERSYN

The days turn into weeks, and I don't hear from Reed. No surprise there. Reed lives and breathes baseball. But his silence still hurts.

I sigh and shove thoughts of Reed to the back of my mind, otherwise, I'll eat through another pint of ice cream, my third in one sitting.

Granger kept his word. When my grandfather and I FaceTime, Granger or his grandmother would poke their heads in view of the camera, and wave or, say "hi."

My grandfather raves about how nice everyone is to him. I didn't tell him what had happened at the sheriff's office, and I asked Granger to put it out there to everyone involved not to mention it to my grandfather before I left Pandora. They were so grateful I saved Mr. Haider's life, they acquiescence.

Ignorance is bliss, and I just want my grandfather to be happy, though he pesters me for the reason I left so suddenly. I told him there was an emergency back in Pendleton. It was the truth.

The Allens cancelled their wedding at the last minute. The soon-to-be Mrs. Allen confessed to being in love with her soon-to-be-husband's older brother. What a hot mess. Andy and I made a ton of calls cancelling orders on items planned for the affair.

And Pendleton U's dean moved up the welcome-back function because of a scheduling conflict. Thank the stars I had Andy and our team's help. The party was a success, and by the end of the night, we were asked to cater at multiple on-campus parties happening the rest of the year. Business is booming.

"I saw on the sports report, Reed missed games. Something about his grandfather in the hospital after having a cardiac arrest."

Andy shoots me a sideways glance, gauging my reaction to her news. We're chilling on the couch watching "The Haunting of Hill House," our latest Netflix binge. Wow, that family has issues.

"Is that so?" I pop popcorn in my mouth, ignoring the ache in my chest.

The annoying ache comes on strong whenever I think of Reed or when his name comes up in my conversations with Andy, Granger or my grandfather. On FaceTime with my grandfather, I also "speak" with Charlie.

He stayed behind to keep an extra eye on Grandfather for me. I miss him like crazy. He barks and smiles. I coo to him like he's a baby. He's my lovebug. I sigh. Andy's right. Technology isn't a substitute for a real connection.

Andy takes a sip of her beer. "Heard anything from him?"

"Same sob story."

"You should text him."

"Isn't there a period after hooking up with a guy that I *shouldn't* contact him?"

"What?!" She faces me and tucks her knees under her with such force, the couch cushions bounce, and my bowl of popcorn goes flying.

"Emersyn Collins, *you* slept with Reed Haider? When? Did you give the attraction at least forty-eight hours to boil over then simmer before you jumped his bones? Or did you let him slide his you-know-what in you for a home run right off the bat?"

I shake my head. This girl.

"We're not chickens out to be slow-roasted," I point out.

"Emmie." She rolls her eyes. "Tell."

"Okay, fine. We had hot and sweaty sex the day you heard his voice over my AirPods."

"Damn it! I knew I'd be too late. You were so out of breath, Em."

I was. His nearness did strange things to my head, my heart, my belly, and my girly parts.

Andy reaches out and taps my hand.

"He'll call or text soon. Playing ball almost every day of the week has got to be difficult."

"But texting or calling only takes a few seconds of his time. Accept it, Andy. I have. He had a taste of what he left behind, and what he got was lacking."

She throws popcorn at me.

"Stop putting yourself down. You're beautiful, smart, and funny. Reed's loss, okay?" She gets up off the couch. "And this weekend, when you walk into that reception hall looking as hot as the sun, you'll be getting some something-something."

She thrusts her hips and smacks at the air. I laugh. She is something else.

"Speaking of getting some action between the sheets, how are things with Granger?"

"We're getting *reacquainted*."

"Is that what you're calling those video chats you two were having while you're half-naked and he's breathing heavy doing god knows what with his hands?"

"Emmie!"

She blushes. I mime giving a blowjob. Her eyes widen. Then she smiles big and throws a pillow at me. Dodging the pillow, I pat the spot next to me, telling her how happy I am that she and Granger got over their misunderstanding.

Apparently, Andy took her friend's place as an escort after her friend was beat up by a guy Andy believed was the boyfriend. In reality, he was the woman's pimp.

Andy got caught up in a police sting, was arrested and in the ensuing chaos, she gave the officers her friend's name. They looked so alike they could be twins. Guess who bailed Andy out of jail after she kicked her boyfriend, aka her pimp, in the balls? Andy's escort friend.

Guess who the "dangerous client with ties to the underworld" was who was in reality an undercover cop? Granger. What a story! And, the icing on the cake? They shared a lustful kiss before the raid went down. No wonder they had looked at one another with longing and suspicion when Andy showed up in Pandora.

It's too bad Granger wasn't there when Andy's friend bailed her out of jail otherwise there would be no misunderstanding.

The episode we're watching ends, and the final episode begins. I slouch into the couch. I'm not looking forward to seeing my ex and his hot AF girlfriend.

She's so hot, she'll be the moon eclipsing my sun.

14

EMERSYN

I sit with my elbow on the table and my chin propped in my palm.

I scan the crowd. Plenty of couples and hardly any single guys in plain sight. Or the single guys are off doing something-something in their car in the back parking lot. Or getting it on in the coat closet. Or having dirty sex in the bathroom stall.

Andy demanded I stop putting myself down, but the reality is there are A LOT of single and beautiful women at Chloe and Mark's wedding.

Speaking of Chloe and Mark, they're slow dancing in the middle of the dance floor to a fast beat, unable to take their eyes and their hands off one another. I smile. Those guys. They're adorable, and I'm happy for them.

Worn out by the sleepless night I had last night, and the nosebleeds I had this afternoon, I shift in my chair and set my head on my crossed arms, not caring that my up-do is coming undone.

"Hi, Miss Emersyn."

I lift my head and peer into big brown eyes.

"Hello, Oliver. Enjoying your sister's wedding?"

"I would enjoy it more if you danced with me."

Wow, so *eloquent*. I raise an eyebrow. "One, how old are you? And two, did Chloe send you over?"

Above his little shoulder, I glimpse my ex and his girlfriend. She's tall and willowy, looking beautiful in a summer dress with spaghetti straps. Her dark hair cascades over her shoulder in rivulets, the ends caressing her mid-back.

She says something funny. Scott laughs and clasps his hand on the small of her back, bringing her flushed against him. A perfect fit. I look away without an ounce of burning jealousy or resentment for his betrayal.

I'm not interested in Scott.

One man still owns a piece of me, the most important part—my heart.

I refocus my attention on little Oliver. He's staring at me in confusion.

"Did you hear anything I said, Miss Emersyn?"

"I will again if you drop the 'Miss.' *And*, I'll dance with you."

"Really?"

"Heck, yes! You're my favorite little man."

He smiles bright. "Well, I'm seven, and no, my sis didn't boss me. I came over on my own."

My eyes tear up. "Thank you, Oliver. That's nice of you."

A new song starts. One that grabs this little guy's soul.

"I love this song. Come on." He grabs my hand and tugs.

I laugh and reach inside my bag. "Let me slip into something better suited for dancing, and we'll dance to our hearts' content."

I take off my heels and put on the ballet flats I stuffed in my bag for when my feet got sore from the heels. I stand and moan at how good it feels to be grounded again.

Oliver yanks me to the middle of the dance floor.

I shake my thang, do the moonwalk, and move my body as though I'm Uma Thurman and Oliver is John Travolta in "Pulp Fiction" to Kriss Kross' "Jump."

"Wow, you can move!" Oliver beams.

God, I love his smile. So pure.

"Thank you, Monsieur."

"What's that mean?"

"Monsieur is French for mister." I grab his hands and swing our arms.

"You speak French?"

I cross my eyes. "I wish."

He laughs more, and I'm in heaven basking in this boy's happiness. He shakes his butt. I shake mine. We whoop and holler. People stare. I ignore them. I couldn't care less if Oliver and I look ridiculous.

Life is too short.

The past is the past and can't be changed.

I'm here to live my best life.

The music ends. Out of breath, I hug Oliver.

"Thank you. Best moment of my night."

"Not yet, it isn't," Andy says from behind me.

I face her. There's a mischievous gleam in her eyes.

The room goes quiet. Then conversation erupts around me.

"Is that the starting pitcher for the Oakland A's?"

"Oh, my God, it is. It's Reed Haider!"

Reed? Reed is *here*?

"He is so hot."

The crowd parts. The star of my sexual fantasies

and the man that owns my heart walks up to me dressed in a plain white T-shirt and low-hung blue jeans.

Goodness, he's smoldering hot. And that wicked smile on his face...

"Hello, Emersyn."

The crowd gasps.

"Reed." I swallow past the tightness in my throat. "Why are you here?"

"I came back for you, sweetheart," he says loud enough for everyone to hear. He shifts his attention to Chloe and Mark. "Congratulations on your wedding, and my apologies for crashing your party."

He takes my hand in his. So warm. So strong. I miss him so much.

"Would you two mind if I steal this beautiful woman away from your special day? You see, it's been non-stop ball for me, and now that I have a breather, I would like to see my girl. I miss her. I love her, too."

"Reed Haider!" My eyes must be wide. My mouth, too.

Reed is known for not passing up an opportunity when the right opportunity presents itself. He kisses me full on the mouth for all to see that I'm his. I'm

Reed Haider's number one girl. His woman. The one he loves.

He loves me.

Reed loves me.

I can't believe this moment is happening.

He breaks off the kiss and looks deep into my eyes. "Ready, Emers?"

I nod, too out of breath to say a word. I follow him out the door and to his truck. I don't question why he has his truck with him. Or that he's in Pendleton rather than Oakland. I don't demand to know how he can love me after what I confessed to have done to his mom that night.

I'm dazed from seeing him again. I'm burning up from the inside out from his scorching hot and very public kiss.

We drive in silence until he parks at a look-out point with a beautiful and clear view of Pendleton below us.

"I've never been here," I say, breaking through the comfortable silence.

"I should hope not. One of my baseball buddies grew up in Pendleton. He said people come here for one reason and one reason only. It's a tradition."

"What is it?" I face him, my cheeks toasty from the heat in his gaze.

"I'm not ready to tell, Emers."

I glance around. The lot is empty. To get here, we had to turn onto a bumpy, dirt road off the main road, the turn obscured by trees and wild clumps of brush.

"How's life?"

Reed's question takes me back to the day he followed me to our secret spot by the creek.

"Life's good, but it could be better. Did you mean what you said back at my friend's wedding?"

"Every word."

"But how can you love me after what I did to your family? How, Reed?"

"Emers."

There's so much love in his voice.

"Come here, babe." He reaches for me. I unbuckle and let him pull me onto his lap.

"I love you so much," I tell him, afraid this moment will end. That I'll wake up, and it's only a dream. "How can you love me?" I ask again.

"You stayed true to who you are, Emersyn Collins. You're kind, strong, protective, stubborn, *and* you keep your promises no matter the consequences."

He grasps my chin and forces me to look him in the eye.

"And that's how I can love you so much I hurt when you're not with me, Em. My grandfather confessed." He sets his forehead on mine. "He told me what happened that night. The secrets and lies you hold inside you for the sake of protecting us and my family…"

He sighs, and it's deep.

I don't like that he hurts for me. I want to take away his emotional pain. But this is our moment to come clean and have a fresh start. I'm certain that's the reason he brought me to this secluded look-out point.

"I understand now why you kept his affair with my mom a secret. You didn't feel it was your secret to tell."

His voice trembles, and I wrap my arms around him, letting him know I'm here for him.

"My mom was my light, always bright and happy. My dad, my biggest supporter, until I made you mine and your words of encouragement made me work harder for what I wanted, a future with you and to play in the Majors. And my grandfather was my rock, my solid foundation. Their betrayal would've destroyed me and my father. And that old bugger dared threaten to destroy *me* with *our* secret. He said he had a picture of a screenshot of our texts."

Anger. Disbelief. Hurt. The emotions chase across Reed's handsome face, and my chest aches. It must have been difficult to hear of his well-respected grandfather's betrayal.

"Yes," I confirm. "He told me he had proof that you and I started having sex when I was sixteen. He threatened to have the authorities go after you for statutory rape. I was so scared, Reed. Your mom fell over. Your grandfather and I reached for her, but it was too late. Then we heard you calling for me, and he panicked."

Raindrops hitting my face.

Reed's grandfather's horror and wailing changing to anger and screaming.

"He demanded I come up with a lie that would put the blame on me and keep his affair with your mom a secret."

I take a shuddering breath, recalling the events leading up to that tragic night. Reed proposing by the creek earlier that day. Me in tears running away from him. Reed and I meeting in secret later that night. Reed demanding an answer. Marry him and leave for California, or break his heart and stay in Pandora?

I asked for more time, but he pushed and pushed. I scrambled out of his truck and ran off into the downpour, needing to distance myself from the decision I already made. A decision I put into words in the letter that didn't make it to Reed.

"I'm sorry for everything." I bunch his shirt in my hands, glad to finally be able to tell him the truth. The truth is complicated but it feels so good to finally let go of all these words that had lived inside me.

However, Reed isn't done going over what happened.

"So your false confession was coerced?"

Was it coercion when I had the choice to defy Reed's grandfather's threats and tell the truth? But the past is the past, and I can't change it no matter how many times I do so in my mind.

I confessed to Reed and the sheriffs that his mom heard the ridiculous rumor Reed and I were meeting in secret. She wanted to discover for herself if there could be a truth to the rumors. She took his grandfather with her, and they searched for our secret spot hidden in the woods near the cliffside.

I ran into them when I ran from Reed. Reed's mom demanded to know the truth. I scoffed at her accusation.

Reed would never look at someone like me once much less twice as girlfriend material. She called me a liar and dug her nails into my arm. I turned and gave her a good shove. She slipped on the wet, soft dirt and fell to her death.

The truth was Reed's mom and his grandfather argued. I overheard her screaming she wanted to divorce Reed's dad and take her relationship with Reed's grandfather public. He refused.

I tip my chin. "I will not be pressing charges against your grandfather if that's where your question is heading. He's old, and I'm ready to put the past behind me. Behind us."

"*Emersyn.*" He sighs.

"I won't see you locked up in jail for what we did as teenagers, Reed Haider."

"We're fine, sweetheart. As soon as my grandfather confessed, I searched the age of consent, and it's sixteen."

Thank the stars. "Are we good now, Reed? Can we put that night behind us? Am I able to visit my grandfather in Pandora?"

"Yes to your second and third question, but for us to be good and right again, you have some explaining to do."

"You forgive me for lying to you? For keeping secrets from you?"

"I do if you'll forgive me for being an ass that

night. I shouldn't have pressured you for an answer. I'm sorry, sweetheart. Had we not argued—"

I press my mouth on his and murmur, "I forgive you, Reed."

I'm ready for our fresh start.

"Thank you, Em. Now if you can be so kind as to explain this."

With his arm securely around me, he tips us forward and opens the glove compartment. Reed reaches inside, and when he pulls out his hand, what he's holding has me gasping for air.

No way.

It can't be.

He has my letter from seven years ago, the letter that Granger told me the rain soaked.

15

REED

*H*er green eyes are wide.

She makes a grab for the letter, but I put it out of her reach.

"Reed Haider, where in the hell did you get that from?"

"Granger," I drawl out his name. I'm a lucky bastard to have a great friend.

"He said the letter got soaked in the rain when his girlfriend sidelined and blindsided him with a breakup. He was to give you the letter before you left for California."

She's adorable as fuck with her eyebrows slanted to her cute nose.

"He found it going through his mother's stuff," I explain. "The letter was in his backpack, mixed in with his mother's junk mail. He grabbed the wrong envelope when he went looking for me."

I hand her the envelope.

She turns it over. Once. Twice. Looks at it like it's lost treasure. It is. It's a priceless reminder from our past.

"Will you read your letter to me, Emers?"

She wears down her bottom lip with her teeth.

"I was sixteen when I wrote this, Reed. I'm not the same person."

"Are you saying I have some other girl's heart, right here?" I take her small hand and press it over my heart.

"Reed." Her face softens.

I cup her face and strum my thumb over the graceful arch of her cheek. I don't like seeing uncertainty on this strong woman's face. It had killed me seeing her plead for forgiveness, security, and kindness for her grandfather from my family and the folks that had hurt them.

"What's in the letter won't change what I feel for you. I love you, Emersyn."

"I love you, too." She turns into my touch.

I kiss her forehead, her eyebrows, and her eyelids when she closes her eyes. I kiss the dip above her upper lip, too. I can't get enough of her. She smiles and hums low in her throat. I cover her mouth with mine and linger, enjoying the softness of her lips.

"I like those kisses," she says against mine.

"I have more for you, but for the rest, I want you naked."

Her eyes flutter open. She glances at the envelope in her hand. "Shall we? Then you can keep your word."

Keep my word.

I need to keep my promise to Granger.

"Emers, there's something I have to tell you before you read the letter."

"What is it?"

"You know those grants and scholarships you got that covered your tuition and room and board?"

She gasps. Her eyes widen. Tears up. "That was you. All you, Reed. You kept your promise to take care of me."

"Yes, babe."

"Thank you, thank you, thank you."

"*Now* I'm ready for the letter. You?"

She smiles. "Yes." She opens the envelope. "Okay, here goes. No funny faces. No eye-roll. Remember, I was sixteen."

"Oh, *I* remember. Prettiest girl I ever met. The

brightest smile. Most beautiful green eyes. Biggest heart. And you're still all that and more."

"Laying it on thick."

I lay a kiss on her kisser before I grovel.

"I'm making up for my shitty behavior. I should have called you sooner, but I had too much to process through my thick skull. And the back-to-back games..." I run my fingers through my hair. "Excuses. Damn excuses. I'm sorry, Em."

I blow out a breath.

"It's okay, Reed. What's important is you're here now."

She's too nice. Too good to me. After everything she's gone through to keep *my* family's secrets *her* secret, I'm ready to spend the rest of my life giving Emersyn Collins the best life she could live.

She pulls out the letter and unfolds it. Her movements are precise. Her expression, thoughtful. She clears her throat before she reads her letter to me. To us.

Dear Reed,

I hope this letter finds you well. Cliché, my greeting, but so is what we have if you think long and hard on it.

We met in secret. You're my Romeo and I'm your Juliet. Our story took a tragic turn too.

I'm sorry for what I did to your mom.

I'm sorry I couldn't save her for you.

If I could I would trade places with her in a heartbeat.

For you.

I care so much for you, Reed.

I only want to protect you.

And if letting go will protect you, then I'm letting you go, Reed Haider.

I'm saying no to your proposal.

We're so young, and the big world out there is waiting for you. Your star will shine bright, I'm certain of it.

And I'll be looking up at the night sky knowing you're looking at the same set of stars too.

We're star-crossed lovers, Reed. That's why we're a cliché. See ☺, I made my way back to my original point. You give me such grief for digressing though I know it's in jest.

My grandfather has two favorite sayings.

1. *The more things change, the more they stay the same.*
2. *Sticks and stones may break my bones, but words can never hurt me.*

I have my own: if you love something, let it go. If it comes back, it's yours. If it doesn't, it never was. I hope someday, you'll find your way back to me. Until then, you'll be forever in my heart.

I'll miss you, Reed.

Yours truly,
Emersyn Collins

"Long and drawn out." She sighs and folds the letter. Swipes at her tears with her fingers. "God, I digressed."

"From the heart, Emers. Nothing straight from your heart and soul is ever long and drawn out to me," I reassure. "Another reason I love you. With me, you've always been honest about your feelings."

"It's because I had to bottle it up around the others. Otherwise everything they believed about my father would be true. I was so angry. So hurt over what they did and said. Then 'we' happened, and you took those awful emotions away, Reed. Until that night shattered us."

"I'm sorry I didn't do more to protect you."

"You forget I wanted it that way. If you came to my defense too much, people would get suspicious that something was going on between us. I would rather have *you* than have your protection. Does that make sense?"

"You would rather have star-crossed than wrestling smack-down?" I waggle my brows.

"Reed."

Her frown turns right-side up, and that's what I was going for.

"No, I get it, babe." I pick her up off my lap and set her on the seat. "Private is how you like to live your life. Public would have brought hell on our heads, on your grandfather's too, and you didn't want that. Pandora is his home. Pandora is *my* family's home. You wanted to keep the peace at the expense of me not being able to shout to the world that you're *my* girl."

I open the truck's door and reach for her.

"I want to change that."

I help her out of my truck, and with the moon and the stars and the city of Pendleton as our backdrop, I get down on one knee with her hand firmly in mine.

"Emersyn Collins, will you do me the honor and be my wife?"

She shoves her fist against her mouth. Cries. My heart beats a fast beat waiting for her answer. She throws her arms around me.

"Yes, yes, yes!"

We tumble to the ground, a tangled mess of arms and legs, mouths, tongues, and teeth. We kiss and kiss until we have to come up for air.

Air is overrated.

"I love you so much."

"I love you too, future Mrs. Haider."

Smiling, I hold her tight and glance up at sparkling green eyes I'm lucky to stare into for the rest of my life.

"What now?" Her fingers skim the side of my face, down my neck, and lingers on my arm, before she slips her hand under my shirt.

Small fingers trench in my chest hair. Glide low to stroke the ridges of my six-pack abs. Goes lower. Even lower.

I groan and remove her hand from my pants. I will not take her on the cold, hard ground. I want her squirming and sighing her release in our new king bed.

I bring her hand to my mouth and kiss each fingertip and across her knuckles, paying extra attention to her ring finger, where an engagement ring will soon sit pretty.

"We head home," I finally say, another groan

edging from between my teeth when she squirms, nestling my dick in her hot spot.

"Oakland?"

"Nope."

"Pandora?"

"Nah," I say, grateful Granger found Emersyn's letter. He said it was a final gift from his mother, a gift from heaven. Granger's mom loved Emers. "Here, Em. I bought us a house in Pendleton."

"What?! Reed." A smile spans her beautiful face.

"I bought us a house in Oakland and Pandora, too, but Pendleton will be home until you decide where you want us to live and raise a family."

"A family? Are you sure? My genetics—"

"I whole-heartedly accept. I love you for you, and I'm done settling for just your heart. I want all of you."

"You won't mind having babies with me?"

"I would love and enjoy very much making babies with you."

She climbs off me, stands, and extends her hand. "I'm holding you to your word, Reed Haider."

Laughing, I put my hand in hers. She helps me up, and shit, she's strong. We collide. We kiss. We were once broken up, that night shattering us, but we're put back together, again.

I found my way back to my heart, my sweet Emersyn.

I help her inside my truck. "Ready for home, love?"

"Yes." Coy smile on her face. "Do you by chance have chocolate cream pie in the fridge?"

"I stacked the entire top shelf high with pie."

She smiles and against my curved mouth, she murmurs, "Then what are we waiting for, Champ?"

Milton Keynes UK
Ingram Content Group UK Ltd.
UKHW031902180324
439638UK00003B/179